To Mary, who knew what it meant to be
a friend and taught me well. I miss you.
—B.J.H.

To my husband, Eddy—thank you for all your
support and always trying to make me laugh.
—O.T.M.

Printed in the United States of America

First Edition

1 3 5 7 9 10 8 6 4 2

F322-8368-0-14240

ISBN 978-1-4847-1797-4

Designed by Tony Fejeran

Visit www.disneybooks.com

Disney FROZEN

An Amazing Snowman

by Barbara Jean Hicks

illustrated by Olga T. Mosqueda

Disney PRESS
New York • Los Angeles

Olaf is not
your everyday
snowman.

He
walks.

He
talks.

He even sings.

But those aren't the only things that make him special!

Olaf is special **because**

he sees the **best in EVERYONE.**

His brother, Marshmallow, is a playful fellow . . .

Sven the reindeer
is forever trying to
kiss his nose . . .

and Queen Elsa and Princess Anna
always use their
royal manners.

Olaf is special
because

he finds
beauty in
every day . . .

and because he dreams.

Olaf dreams about sand castles . . .

and ships sailing to new horizons . . .

and swimming with friendly sea creatures.

"Hi there!"

Olaf dreams about soaring in the SKY . . .

and picking fresh fruit . . .

Olaf is special because in his eyes, summer

or
winter,

every day is an
adventure . . .

and
every
night
shines.

Olaf is
special because
he knows
that every
ending . . .

is a chance for a new beginning . . .

and
a
chance . . .

for a
nice, warm
hug!

The
End.